Dirty Bertie

ZOMBIE!

For Miss Menendez and the children of the
Colegio Ingles de Asturias ~ D R
For all the children and staff at Beck Primary
School ~ A M

STRIPES PUBLISHING
An imprint of Little Tiger Press
1 The Coda Centre, 189 Munster Road,
London SW6 6AW

A paperback original
First published in Great Britain in 2013

Characters created by David Roberts
Text copyright © Alan MacDonald, 2013
Illustrations copyright © David Roberts, 2013

ISBN: 978-1-84715-386-9

The right of Alan MacDonald and David Roberts to
be identified as the author and illustrator of this work
respectively has been asserted by them in accordance
with the Copyright, Designs and Patents Act, 1988.

Printed and bound in the UK

10 9 8 7 6 5 4 3

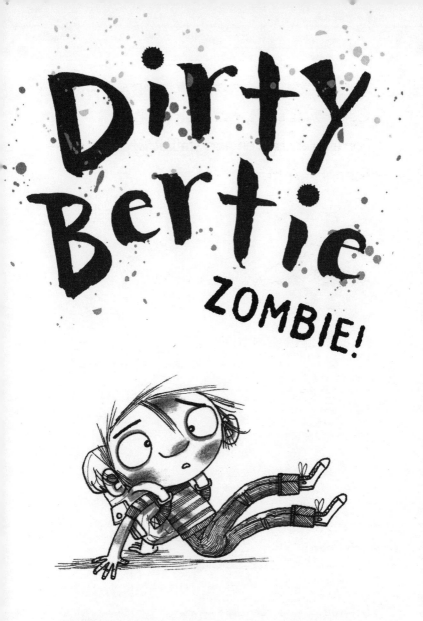

Dirty Bertie
ZOMBIE!

DAVID ROBERTS WRITTEN BY ALAN MACDONALD

Collect all the
Dirty Bertie books!

Contents

CHAPTER 1

Mum came off the phone.

"That was Eugene's mum," she said. "They're going away for the weekend so she's asked if Eugene can stay with us."

Bertie looked up. "You mean for a sleepover?"

Mum nodded.

"Yessss!" yelled Bertie, showering the

table with toast crumbs.

"What about me?" grumbled Suzy. "Don't I get a sleepover?"

"Not this time," said Mum. "It's only Eugene, you'll hardly notice him."

Bertie stuck out his tongue. A whole weekend! This was going to be great. They could stay up late, build a den, make the world's stinkiest stink bomb … but hold on…

"What about Darren?" he said. "Isn't he coming too?"

Mum shook her head. "One friend's enough," she said.

"But I've got *two* friends," argued Bertie. "I can't leave Darren out."

It wouldn't be right. They were the famous three. The three desperados – they always stuck together.

Dirty Bertie

Bertie clasped his hands. "Please! Just this once!" he begged.

Mum sighed. She guessed one more wouldn't make much difference.

"All right!" she said. "But no staying up till all hours of the night."

"We won't," promised Bertie.

A sleepover with his two best friends for a whole weekend! This was going to be *epic*!

Darren and Eugene arrived on Friday night with their sleeping bags. Eugene had a gift from his mum – one of her famous chocolate cakes. Bertie's eyes lit up.

"Uh-uh, don't touch," warned Mum. "We'll save this for Sunday tea."

Bertie took his friends up to his room. He had even tidied up – at least he'd swept his toys under the bed, which was the same thing.

Eugene and Darren unpacked their bags. Bertie picked up a computer game lying on top of Darren's sleeping bag.

"What's this?" he asked.

"*Zap the Zombie!* Haven't you played it?"

Bertie and Eugene shook their heads.

"It's the best game ever," said Darren. "You have to splat the zombies in the haunted house before they disappear."

"Zombies give me nightmares," said Eugene anxiously.

"They're only cartoons," said Darren. "Anyway, you'll love it."

ZIP! ZOOP! SPLAT!

"Yahoo!" cried Bertie as another zombie was splatted.

Mum poked her head into the lounge. "What's all the noise?"

"It's just a game," said Bertie.

"It's brilliant!" said Darren. ZOOP!

"*Zap the Zombie*? Where did you get this?" asked Mum, inspecting the box.

Dirty Bertie

"Darren brought it," replied Bertie.

Mum turned off the TV. "You're not playing that," she said. "It looks completely revolting."

"But Mum…" moaned Bertie.

"No buts. I don't want you getting nightmares. Why don't you play Snap?"

She swept out, taking the zombie game with her. There was a gloomy silence.

"Nightmares! As if!" said Bertie.

CHAPTER 2

CREAK! CREAK!

Bertie and his friends crept down the stairs. It was ten o'clock and they were on a raid. Mum and Dad were watching TV in the lounge. Suzy was in bed.

"Hurry up!" whispered Bertie.

They tiptoed past the lounge and stole into the kitchen. Bertie opened the fridge door. The chocolate cake was on the top shelf.

CLICK! The kitchen light went on.

"Can I help you?" asked Mum.

"We were just … er … getting a drink," gulped Bertie.

"Yes," said Darren. "Eugene was thirsty, weren't you?"

"Was I?" said Eugene.

"Well, you won't find squash in the fridge," said Mum. "And if you're after chocolate cake, forget it. It's for Sunday tea."

Bertie closed the fridge door. "But we can't get to sleep!" he moaned.

"Try staying in bed," said Mum.

"We're starving!" pleaded Bertie.

Mum rolled her eyes. "Go back to bed. I'll bring you some snacks in a minute."

Snacks! Brilliant! thought Bertie. He knew for certain there were Monster Munchie bars in the cupboard.

Five minutes later Mum knocked on the door. She set down a plate.

"Fruit?" groaned Bertie.

"It's good for you," said Mum. "Far better than crisps or chocolate!"

"I like fruit!" said Eugene.

It didn't take long to empty the plate.

Eugene helped himself to a piece of orange. "EWWW!" he cried, taking a bite. "This orange is RED!"

Darren looked up. "You didn't eat that, did you? It's a *blood orange!*" he gasped.

"Is that bad?" asked Eugene.

"Bad? It's full of BLOOD!" said Darren, winking at Bertie.

"No it isn't," said Eugene.

"Of course it is," said Darren. "If you drink blood juice you'll turn into a *zombie!*"

Eugene frowned. "You're making it up," he said.

"Ask Bertie," said Darren.

Bertie nodded. "Darren's right. How much did you eat? Not all of it?"

Eugene pushed the plate away. He was certain they were trying to trick him. All the same, he wished he hadn't eaten that orange.

"There's no such thing as zombies," he said, getting into his sleeping bag.

17

Dirty Bertie

He snuggled down inside. How did you know if you were turning into a zombie? Did your face turn brown and wrinkly like a prune? He hoped he was going to sleep tonight.

CHAPTER 3

RATTLE, RATTLE, RATTLE!

Bertie woke up. What was that noise?

He sat up in bed. In the dark, he could just make out Eugene trying to open the bedroom door.

"Eugene?" whispered Bertie.

Eugene didn't answer. Finally he got the door open and vanished into

Dirty Bertie

the darkness. Bertie stared after him.
If Eugene needed the toilet why didn't
he turn on the landing light? Bertie crept
out on to the landing.

CREAK! CREAK!

Eugene was heading downstairs.

"Hey, Eugene!" hissed Bertie. "Where
are you going?"

Eugene didn't reply. He carried on
plodding downstairs as if he was
in a dream. Bertie followed
him down to the kitchen
and found him standing
in the dark. He seemed
to have forgotten
why he was
there.

Dirty Bertie

"Eugene? You're giving me the creeps," said Bertie.

Eugene turned and looked right through him as if he wasn't there.

Suddenly the ghastly truth dawned on Bertie. The dead eyes, the silence, the gormless expression – it all made sense… *Eugene had turned into a ZOMBIE!*

Bertie backed away. Zombies were always hungry … what if he tried to— Wait, Eugene was opening the fridge door. He brought out his mum's chocolate cake. Bertie's eyes widened. Surely he wasn't going to…

"UMMMMF!"

Eugene sank his teeth into the cake.

Dirty Bertie

Yikes! thought Bertie. He didn't know zombies ate chocolate cake. Eugene wiped his mouth on the back of his hand and returned the cake to the fridge. Then he left the kitchen, almost walking straight into Bertie.

Upstairs, Bertie watched as Eugene climbed into his sleeping bag and instantly fell asleep. It was weird! Eugene had never done anything like this before. Bertie lay awake for a long time, keeping a careful eye on him. *One thing's for sure,* he thought, *I'm never eating blood oranges!*

Next morning, Eugene acted as if nothing out of the ordinary had happened. At breakfast Bertie watched him pour Chocco Pops into a bowl.

"So how are you feeling?" Bertie asked. "Sleep okay?"

"Fine," said Eugene, reaching for the milk.

"You don't remember anything about last night?"

"I remember you and Darren trying to trick me," grinned Eugene. "Zombies! As if!"

Mum appeared in her dressing gown. She opened the fridge door and gasped.

Uh oh, thought Bertie.

Mum stared at the chocolate cake, which had a large bite-size chunk missing. She lifted it out and glared at Bertie. "Did *you* do this?"

"*Me?*" said Bertie. "No!"

"I told you not to touch it," said Mum.

"But I didn't!" said Bertie.

"Then who did?"

"Eugene!" said Bertie, truthfully.

Eugene looked up. "ME?"

"Don't tell lies, Bertie," snapped Mum.

"I'm not!" said Bertie. "Last night he turned into a zombie and ate a big bit of cake!"

Mum snorted. "You expect me to believe that? I warned you this was for Sunday. I've a good mind not to let you have any."

She put the cake back in the fridge and stormed out.

Darren sniggered. "Ha ha! Good one, Bertie!"

"It wasn't *me!* It was Eugene," cried Bertie.

Eugene frowned. "I don't know why you're trying to blame me," he said crossly. "I was asleep the whole time!"

While Eugene was cleaning his teeth, Bertie grabbed Darren and shut the bedroom door. They needed to talk.

"Listen, I'm not making it up," said Bertie. "Last night Eugene turned into a zombie!"

"Ha ha! Right!" chortled Darren.

"I'm *serious!*" cried Bertie. "It must've

been that blood orange."

"That was a joke," said Darren. "You don't become a zombie by eating an orange!"

"Well, Eugene did," said Bertie. "You didn't see him in the middle of the night. He was acting weird!"

Darren frowned. "He seems all right now."

"I know," admitted Bertie. "But there's only one way to find out."

"What's that?" said Darren.

Bertie lowered his voice. "We'll have to stay awake tonight and see if he does it again."

CHAPTER 4

DONG! DONG! DONG!

The clock in the hall struck midnight. Bertie had been lying awake for hours. Loud snores came from the next sleeping bag. Darren was useless, he'd barely stayed awake for five minutes.

THUMP!

Bertie sat up. It was starting – Eugene

was off on his travels once more! Bertie watched him open the door and slip out of the room. He leaned over and shook Darren by the shoulder.

"Wake up!" he hissed. "He's at it again."

This time Bertie was prepared. He'd hidden a torch under his pillow so they wouldn't have to blunder around in the dark. They followed Eugene downstairs.

Darren stopped. "Wait, what if he attacks us?" he whispered.

"It's only Eugene," said Bertie.

"Yes, but zombies have the strength of ten men," said Darren.

"Don't worry, last night he didn't even know I was there," said Bertie.

They pushed opened the door to the kitchen. Eugene was sitting at the table

Dirty Bertie

in the dark. He had a knife and fork, and the chocolate cake in front of him.

"Hi, Eugene, what's up?" said Darren.

"He can't hear you," whispered Bertie, waving a hand in front of Eugene's face. "He's in zombie world."

Eugene suddenly spoke, making them both jump.

"I've laid the table," he said.

Dirty Bertie

Bertie and Darren looked at each other. It seemed safest to play along and sit down. Eugene cut a fat slice of cake and crammed it into his mouth in one go.

"Crumbs! He's pretty greedy for a zombie!" said Darren.

"At least Mum can't blame me this time," said Bertie.

Upstairs Mum was awake, sitting up in bed. She shook Dad by the arm.

"Listen! Someone's downstairs!" she hissed.

Dad rolled over. They both listened for a few moments. There were definitely voices.

"Burglars?" said Dad.

Dirty Bertie

"You better go and see," whispered Mum.

"Me?"

"Well, I'm not doing it!"

Dad looked in the cupboard and found one of his old golf clubs. He crept downstairs clutching it, while Mum followed at a safe distance. They could hear the intruders in the kitchen.

"Go on!" hissed Mum.

Dad gripped the golf club. He was sure you weren't meant to tackle burglars – right now he'd rather be hiding under the bed.

Dirty Bertie

He kicked open the door and rushed in.

"YAAARGHH!"

"AAARGHH!"

Two of the burglars jumped to their feet. It was dark but they seemed to be wearing pyjamas.

"Don't move! I'm calling the police!" yelled Dad. He wished he was holding his phone instead of a golf club.

"DAD! IT'S ME!" cried Bertie, switching on the light.

Mum and Dad stared.

"Bertie! You scared us half to death!" groaned Mum.

"What are you doing down here?" said Dad.

"Following Eugene," said Bertie. "I told you, he's turned into a zombie!"

They all looked at Eugene who hadn't moved from his seat. He was on his second slice of chocolate cake.

Mum gasped. "He's not a zombie, he's sleepwalking!"

"What?" said Bertie.

"It's happened before. His mum mentioned it on the phone."

This was news to Bertie.

"Why didn't you tell us?" he said.

Mum shrugged. "I forgot all about it."

"Well, shouldn't we wake him up?" asked Dad.

Mum shook her head firmly. "No, that's the last thing you should do."

Just then, Eugene suddenly stood up and walked past them. They followed him upstairs where he climbed into bed. Unfortunately it wasn't *his* bed.

Dad groaned. "Now what? He can't sleep in our bed."

"He'll have to," said Mum. "We mustn't wake him."

"Then what do we do?" asked Dad. "It's almost one in the morning!"

"I know!" cried Bertie. "We could play *Zap the Zombie!*"

Dirty Bertie

"At the window!"

"Quick!"

"Get him!"

ZAP! SPLAT!

"Yesss!" shouted Mum as another zombie bit the dust.

Bertie high fived Darren and his parents. This was turning out to be the best sleepover ever!

CHAPTER 1

"Hurry up, Bertie!" sighed Mum.

"You'll make us late," moaned Suzy.

Bertie trailed after them into the
leisure centre. Saturday morning and his
mum had dragged him along to watch
Suzy's dance class. Could anything be
more boring? Why couldn't Suzy choose
something interesting — like karate or

skydiving? Bertie wouldn't have minded watching that. But dance – he'd rather be doing his homework. At least he didn't have to take part. That would be torture!

"Bertie, get a move on!" grumbled Mum.

They reached the hall. Miss Foxtrot's dance class stood around in puffy tutus and tights, pointing their toes.

Dirty Bertie

Bertie flopped into a seat beside his mum. Uh oh, Miss Foxtrot was coming over. She was tall and thin, like an ostrich in a cardigan.

"And who is this young man?" she asked.

"Oh. This is Suzy's brother, Bertie," replied Mum.

"And does he like dancing?" asked Miss Foxtrot.

"NO, he doesn't," said Suzy firmly.

"I've just come to watch," said Bertie.

Actually he'd come because his mum had made him.

"Nonsense!" clucked Miss Foxtrot. "You won't learn anything by watching. You must join in!"

Join in? Bertie almost choked. "It's okay, I'll just sit here," he said.

But Miss Foxtrot was dragging him up by the arm. "Don't be silly, there's no need to be shy," she said.

"I'm not! I can't dance," said Bertie desperately. "I don't have the right shoes."

"Don't worry," smiled Miss Foxtrot, "I always keep a spare pair, just in case." She dangled a pair of ballet shoes before him. They were pink – the same colour as Bertie's face.

"I … I can't!" he gasped.

"Really, he'd better not," said Mum.

"He'll just get in the way," said Suzy.

Dirty Bertie

But Miss Foxtrot was already helping Bertie on with the ballet shoes.

Bertie stared at his feet in horror. This was turning into the worst day of his life. What if anyone from school saw him dancing – with a class of girls? It didn't bear thinking about!

Suzy hissed in his ear. "Don't you *dare* mess this up!"

Bertie stuck out his tongue. Hang on, that gave him an idea. Maybe if he messed up, Miss Foxtrot wouldn't want him in her class…

"Places, children, places!" cried the teacher, clapping her hands. She pressed a button and syrupy music began to play.

"Let's begin by making ourselves *ever so* small!" trilled Miss Foxtrot. "Imagine you are teeny, tiny seeds in the earth."

The class obeyed, curling up small.

"Teeny, Bertie, not droopy!" frowned Miss Foxtrot. "Now, with the music, slowly start to grow. Up, up, spread your leaves to the sun!"

Bertie grew bigger – and bigger. He grew into a giant. A huge, angry giant stamping on the ants in his way…

"OWW!" cried Kylie.

"ARGHH!" yelled Flora.

"Bertie kicked me!" howled Smeeta, clutching her leg.

"BERTIE!" screeched Miss Foxtrot. The music skidded to a halt.

"Yes?"

"That is NOT how we behave in class! Go and wait outside!"

Bertie smiled to himself. Dance lessons were over for the day. He left the ballet slippers on the floor and headed for the door. The row of parents glared after him.

"Can I get a drink?" he asked his mum.

"No!"

"Can I borrow your phone then?" begged Bertie. "Just to play one game."

Mum handed it over. "Try to stay out of trouble," she sighed.

Bertie sat against the wall playing *Wacky Worm Racer* on his mum's mobile. Suzy's dance class had been going on for hours. He wandered down the corridor to look in the other rooms.

The first one had a toddler group singing nursery rhymes. The second had a yoga class tying themselves in knots. From the last room came the sound of loud, thumping music. Bertie looked in and saw rows of women stomping

Dirty Bertie

to the beat. Some of them were as old as his mum! He pressed his nose to the glass. His eyes grew round. No, it couldn't be! It was! In the back row, wearing an orange leotard and stripey leggings, was Miss Boot, his teacher!

CHAPTER 2

Bertie's mouth hung open. This was the funniest thing he'd ever seen. Miss Boot, the terror of the school, the scourge of Class 3, *Miss Boot* was in there dancing! And not just dancing but panting, sweating and waving her arms as if she'd just scored a goal.

Bertie had never considered what

Dirty Bertie

Miss Boot did out of school. Surely teachers just ate and slept and shouted at children? But it turned out he was wrong – Miss Boot had a hobby…

Bertie had never heard of Zumba. It seemed to be crazy dancing for old people. He watched as Miss Boot tried to copy the dance teacher. She kicked up

Dirty Bertie

her legs. She side-stepped to the right.
She spun round like a top and found
herself facing the wrong way. Her face
was red as a beetroot and dripping
with sweat.

Bertie shook his head. This was
hilarious! If only his friends were here to
see it too!

Wait a moment, he thought. *Darren's house is only five minutes away.* He could use his mum's mobile! He punched in the number.

"Hello?"

"Darren, it's me!" cried Bertie.

"Hey, Bertie, what's up?"

Darren sounded like he was eating something.

"You'll never believe it," said Bertie. "I'm at the leisure centre. You've got to get down here now."

"I can't. I'm having breakfast," said Darren.

"Trust me, you don't want to miss this," said Bertie. "Oh, and bring a camera."

"What for?" asked Darren.

"Never mind, just do it," said Bertie. "And hurry up!"

Dirty Bertie

Ten minutes later, Darren arrived. He was out of breath and had obviously dressed in a hurry.

"Have you got it?" asked Bertie.

"What?"

"The camera of course!"

"In my pocket," said Darren. "Why? What's going on?"

Bertie led him to the door and they pressed their noses to the glass.

"DANCING?" said Darren. "You dragged me all the way here to see dancing?"

Bertie shook his head. "Look," he said. "The one at the back in the stripey leggings."

Darren looked again. He gasped.

Dirty Bertie

"NOOOO! IT ISN'T!" he cried.

Bertie grinned. "It is. It's Miss Boot!" he said. "Now you see why I called you?"

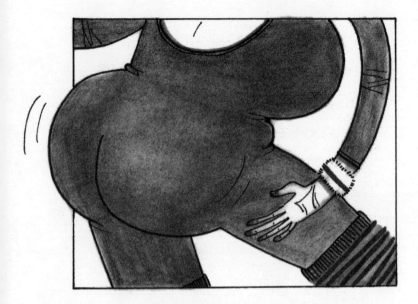

CHAPTER 3

The two boys watched with their breath steaming up the glass. Inside the room the beat was growing faster.

BOOM! BOOM! BOOM! BOOM!

"Let's go!" cried the Zumba teacher. "Let me see you shake it!"

The class began to sway and wiggle their hips. Miss Boot was waggling her

Dirty Bertie

bottom as if she had ants in her pants.
She raised one arm, pointing to the sky.

BOOM! BOOM! BOOM!

"She's bonkers!" hooted Bertie.

"She's potty!" said Darren.

They danced up and down the
corridor, copying Miss Boot.

"Shake it! Shake it!" cried Darren,
wobbling like a jelly.

"Move it, move it!" shouted
Bertie, sticking out his
bottom.

They bumped into each other
and collapsed on the floor, in fits of
giggles.

"Ha ha! Hee hee!" snorted Darren.
"If only people at school could see this!"

"They can," said Bertie.

Darren looked at him. "How do you
mean?"

"That's why we need the camera,
dimbo!" said Bertie. "To take a picture of
Miss Boot dancing like a fruitcake."

It took a moment for Darren to get it.
His face broke into a huge grin.

"Wicked!" he cried. "Wait till we
show Eugene."

"We could pin it up in class," said
Bertie.

"It'll be the best joke ever!"

"It'll go down in history!"

Imagine Miss Boot's face when she saw herself. There was only one small problem.

"Who's taking the picture?" asked Bertie.

Darren's smile melted away. "Not me!"

"It's your camera," said Bertie.

"Yeah, but it's *your* idea," argued Darren.

Bertie looked through the door. "What if we took the photo from out here?" he said.

"It won't work," said Darren. "You've got to get close or you won't know it's her."

"Well, I'm not going in there," said Bertie. "She'll eat me alive!"

"Not if she doesn't know it's you," said Darren. "Put your hood up. All you have to do is dash in, get the picture and leg it."

Bertie frowned. "If it's that easy, why don't you do it?" he said.

"Someone's got to hold the door," said Darren.

BOOM! BOOM! BOOM! The music thumped on. It was no use standing there arguing. If they waited too long the class would end and they'd lose their chance. One of them had to risk it and clearly it wasn't going to be Darren.

Bertie sighed and put up his hood. Why was it always him?

Darren handed him the camera. "Just press this button," he said. "It's dead easy."

Bertie took a last look through the window. The Zumba class seemed to be

Dirty Bertie

working up a sweat. Miss Boot's face had gone purple. She looked as if she might pass out. Bertie took a deep breath. *Here goes…*

BOOM! BOOM! BOOM! The music thumped louder as Darren opened the door.

Bertie dashed in, keeping his head down, and raised the camera. The class had their backs to him. But at that moment Miss Boot spun round. Her mouth gaped open like a fish…

SNAP!

Bertie bolted out of the door. Darren slammed it shut and they both raced down the corridor at top speed.

"Well, did you get it?" panted Darren.

Bertie nodded and handed over the camera. It had all happened in a blur. For all he knew he'd taken a picture of his own feet!

Darren pressed a button. His eyes lit up. "Wicked!" he said. "Wait till they see this at school!"

CHAPTER 4

Miss Boot marched into Class 3 and put down her bag. It was a Monday morning like any other. But something wasn't right. Her class were all staring at her as if she'd grown two heads. Half of them wore idiotic grins on their faces. Others were giggling. In the back row Bertie and Darren looked like they might explode.

Miss Boot folded her arms. "Well? What is it? Would someone like to share the joke?"

No one spoke.

"Very well," said Miss Boot sternly. "Settle down and let's get on with our work."

She turned to the board to write today's date. She gasped. Her face turned white. On the board was a photo – *a photo of HER at Zumba class!* She looked like a madwoman in a leotard.

"Hee! Hee! Hee!"

A new wave of giggles broke out. Miss Boot glowered. Someone was going to suffer for this. She tore down the photo and held it up.

"SILENCE!" she barked. "WHO DID THIS? WHO IS RESPONSIBLE?"

Dirty Bertie

None of the class met her eye. Miss Boot's gaze swept over them, seeking out the guilty one. In the back row, Eugene's shoulders were shaking. Darren had his fist jammed in his mouth. Bertie was laughing so much his nose was running like a tap.

Miss Boot narrowed her eyes. She remembered the boy who'd burst into her Zumba class. He had a camera and was wearing a brown hoodie – just like the one Bertie was wearing now. She smiled a thin smile.

"BERTIE," she said.

Uh oh, thought Bertie.

"Me, Miss?"

"Yes, you, Bertie. Come here."

Bertie trailed up to the front.

Miss Boot pushed the photo under his

nose. "Did you take this picture, Bertie?"
she demanded.

"Me?" gulped Bertie.

"That's what I asked. DID-YOU-
TAKE-THIS-PICTURE?"

Miss Boot's eyes were hypnotizing
him. He couldn't look away.

"SPEAK UP!" bawled Miss Boot.

Bertie gave a slight nod.

Miss Boot crumpled the photo in her hand. "So, you like dancing, do you?" she said.

"Not really," said Bertie.

"Oh, I think you do, since you're so fond of taking pictures of it," said Miss Boot. "Well, I have a little treat for you. Run along and join Miss Darling's class in the hall."

Dirty Bertie

"Miss Darling's class?" said Bertie. They were Class 1 – the baby class. Why did Miss Boot want him to join them?

As Bertie got closer to the hall, the sound of jolly music reached his ears. Miss Darling's class were lined up in two rows, the boys facing the girls.

"Bertie!" cried Miss Darling. "Can I help you?"

"Um … Miss Boot sent me," mumbled Bertie.

"Lovely!" beamed Miss Darling. "We were just about to start country dancing. I think Angela needs a partner, don't you, Angela?"

Angela nodded happily and held out a hand.

Bertie backed away. Country dancing? With Angela? Noooo! How could Miss Boot do this to him?

ZOO!

CHAPTER 1

Bertie gazed out of the window as the coach entered the gates. This was it – *the zoo* – the greatest school trip ever! He couldn't wait to get inside. He wanted to see everything – the lions, tigers, bears, gorillas, hippos and, best of all, the elephants.

Last week, Miss Boot had asked the class to choose an animal and make

Dirty Bertie

a Fact File. Bertie had picked elephants.
He'd drawn a massive elephant poo
beside a pigeon dropping. Miss Boot had
written, "See me!" in his book.

The coach stopped and Bertie joined
the stampede to get off. But the huge
figure of Miss Boot blocked the gangway.

"STOP! Everyone back to their seats!"
she yelled.

The class groaned.

"Before we go anywhere, let me remind you of the rules. First of all, keep together, I don't want anyone getting lost. Secondly, no running, no yelling and no fighting."

Bertie rolled his eyes. *In other words, no fun*, he thought.

"Finally, DO NOT feed the animals," warned Miss Boot. "And I'm talking to you, Bertie."

Bertie gaped. He wasn't going to feed the animals – not unless Know-All Nick leaned over the crocodile pool.

Nick raised his hand.

"Can we make sketches, Miss?"

"Excellent idea, Nicholas," said Miss Boot. She sighed. Bertie was waving an arm. "What is it?"

"When can we eat our lunch?" asked
Bertie.

"When I say so and not before,"
snapped Miss Boot.

They waited at the entrance while Miss
Boot collected the tickets. Bertie wished
they didn't have to stay together. He
wanted to race off and find the elephant
house. Maybe the zookeeper would let
him climb up for a ride? If he had a pet
elephant he'd train it to pick up heavy
objects – Miss Boot, for instance.

Finally they set off with Miss Boot
and Mr Weakly leading the way. Bertie,
Darren and Eugene kept to the back.
Miss Boot dragged them round all the
boring bits of the zoo. They saw a camel

chewing grass, a flock of deer and a yak dozing in the sun.

Bertie sighed. When were they going to see the lions and elephants? He didn't want to miss feeding time – and, talking of food, he was starving!

"When's lunch?" he moaned.

"Not for hours," said Eugene.

"And Miss Boot says you've got to wait," said Know-All Nick, butting in.

"Who asked you, smelly?" said Bertie. Nick was such a teacher's pet. He probably didn't pick his nose without permission. Well, Bertie couldn't wait any longer – he reached into his rucksack for his lunch box.

"Umm, you're not allowed!" cried Nick.

"It's *my* lunch," said Bertie.

"But Miss Boot said you mustn't," bleated Nick. "I'm telling!"

Bertie took no notice. His mum had packed him two rolls. Cheese and peanut butter – yum! But as he went to take a bite, Nick snatched it from him.

"HEY! Give that back!" shouted Bertie.

"Make me, bogey nose!" jeered Nick.

Bertie made a grab for the roll but Nick threw it to Trevor and missed. It sailed right over his head, landing on

Dirty Bertie

the other side of some railings.

"Oops! Silly me!" smirked Nick.

Bertie glared in fury. "Go and get it!"

"I can't," said Nick. "Look where it is."

Bertie looked. The railings were actually part of the monkey cage. Over by their house, a group of monkeys were playing on some rubber tyres. Bertie scowled. He would get Nick for this.

CHAPTER 2

Bertie could see his roll lying just inside the railings. It was probably dirty but who cared about that?

"You could reach it," he told Nick.

"Reach it yourself!" Nick replied.

"*You* threw it," said Bertie.

"Tough luck!" sneered Nick. "Serves you right for being such a greedy pig!"

Dirty Bertie

Bertie scowled. If he had his way, Nick would be locked in a cage and never let out. He glanced round.

Miss Boot was up ahead, admiring the flamingos with the rest of the class. No one was watching. Bertie reached a hand through the bars. The roll was just out of reach. Maybe if he squeezed his head through? Got it! Now to get out before Miss Boot or the monkeys noticed.

UHHHH? Bertie tried to free his head. ARGH! HE WAS STUCK!

Dirty Bertie

He tried turning his head one way then the other. It made no difference – it wouldn't fit through. He was starting to panic.

"What are you playing at?" asked Know-All Nick behind him.

"I'm stuck!" grunted Bertie.

"Oh dear!" sniggered Nick. "Shall I fetch Miss Boot?"

"NO! Just get me out!" cried Bertie.

Nick folded his arms. "Hmm, let me think about that," he said.

Darren and Eugene came over.

"What's going on?" asked Darren.

"Bertie's got his head stuck," crowed Nick. "It's because it's so big."

"You're kidding," said Darren.

"Stop messing around," said Eugene.

"I'M NOT!" moaned Bertie. "DO something!"

Darren and Eugene looked at each other. Miss Boot wasn't going to like this. Any minute now she might see Bertie and march over.

"Turn your head," urged Eugene.

"I've tried that!" said Bertie.

"Hold your breath and count to fifty," said Darren.

Bertie rolled his eyes. "That's for hiccups!"

"I've got an idea!" chortled Nick.

Dirty Bertie

"Let's tickle his feet!"

Bertie ground his teeth. If he ever got out of this he'd get even with that two-faced sneak. He'd push him in an elephant poo. He'd put a rattlesnake down his trousers. He'd...

"OWWW! What are you doing?"

"Trying to get you out," said Eugene. He and Darren pulled with all their might.

Dirty Bertie

"ARGHHH!" yelled Bertie. "YOU'LL PULL MY HEAD OFF!"

They let go. Up ahead, Miss Boot had finished talking and the class were moving off.

"Bye Bertie, have fun!" cried Nick, hurrying to catch up.

Eugene looked round. "We'll have to go," he said.

"Hang on!" cried Bertie. "You can't just leave me!"

"We can't all stay," said Darren. "Miss Boot will notice if we're missing."

"But what if I'm attacked by monkeys?" moaned Bertie.

Darren looked over. The monkeys were busy swinging on their tyres.

"You'll be okay," he said. "Good job it's not the lions' den – that *would* be bad."

Dirty Bertie

"We'll come back later," said Eugene.

"WAIT!" cried Bertie. "You can't just—"

But they'd gone. He was left alone. Actually not quite alone because one of the monkeys was looking at him with bright little eyes. It threw back its head and screeched.

Uh oh, thought Bertie. *Just when I thought things couldn't get any worse.*

CHAPTER 3

The monkeys were coming over. There were five of them with curly tails and wrinkled old men's faces.

"Hi," gulped Bertie. "It's okay … um, I won't hurt you."

"EEEH EEEH EEEEEH!" screeched the smallest monkey. He had tiny teeth which looked as sharp as needles.

"I'm stuck," explained Bertie. He offered the bread roll. "Anyone like cheese and peanut butter?"

The small monkey crept closer and suddenly made a grab for the roll. He scampered away holding it in his paws. This led to a fight with screeching and rolling around in the dirt. At last the small monkey escaped with his prize. The others chased him but he leaped out of their reach.

"HEY! GET OFF!" cried Bertie.

The monkey was perched on his head, clutching his cheese and peanut butter roll. *This is getting ridiculous*, thought Bertie. *Now I'm being used as a picnic table!*

Dirty Bertie

Meanwhile, the rest of the class were watching the penguins dive-bomb their pool.

"Do you think Bertie's all right?" Eugene whispered.

"He'll be fine," said Darren. "We'll check on him later."

Eugene couldn't help worrying. What if they couldn't go back for him? What if the coach drove off leaving Bertie behind? He might be stuck there all night. He might be stuck there forever!

Miss Boot stood over them, doing a headcount.

"Twenty-seven, twenty-eight, twenty-nine…"

Someone was missing. She groaned. How many times had she told them to

stay together? She ran through the list of
likely suspects. Darren – here, Royston
– here, Bertie… Where was Bertie?
She might have known. He'd probably
wandered off to the reptile house or
somewhere.

"Where's Bertie?" she asked Eugene.

Eugene turned scarlet. "Oh, um …
isn't he here?" he mumbled.

"No, he's not," said Miss Boot.
She raised her voice. "Has anyone seen
Bertie?"

A hand went up.

"I have," said Know-All Nick. "He was at the monkey cage."

Miss Boot frowned. "Why didn't you say so? What's he doing there?"

"He's stuck," said Nick.

"STUCK? What do you mean *stuck*?"

"In the railings – he's got his head stuck," said Nick, sounding pleased.

Miss Boot closed her eyes. It was going to be one of those days.

CHAPTER 4

Back at the monkey enclosure a small crowd had gathered. People wanted to see the boy with his head stuck. The monkey on Bertie's head had finished the roll and was now searching for fleas in Bertie's hair. Everyone was staring. Bertie wanted to die. One or two people were taking his picture while they waited for a zookeeper to arrive.

"BERTIE!" thundered a voice. "What are you doing?"

Bertie groaned. Miss Boot – that was all he needed.

"I'm stuck!" he wailed.

"Don't be stupid. If you got your head in there then you can get it out!"

"I can't," moaned Bertie. "I've tried!"

"Well, try harder," snapped Miss Boot. "Nicholas, come and help me."

Miss Boot seized hold of Bertie's left leg while Nick grabbed the right. They pulled as if he was a Christmas cracker.

"OWWWW! THAT HURTS!" yelled
Bertie.

They let go. It was no use.

"Shall I call the fire brigade?" offered
Nick.

"Don't be ridiculous," snapped Miss
Boot.

Just then a zookeeper pushed through
the crowd.

"What's the trouble?" he asked.

"It's his head," explained Miss Boot.
"Goodness knows how he did it – with
Bertie nothing surprises me."

The zookeeper crouched down
beside Bertie. "Okay chief, are you all
right?" he smiled.

All right? thought Bertie. Did he look
all right?

"Get me out," he croaked.

"Don't panic, we will," said the zookeeper.

The crowd watched him take out his keys and open the cage door. The monkey on Bertie's head whooped and jumped off to join his friends.

"Hmm, this is going to be tricky," said the zookeeper. "I might need my hacksaw."

"*Hacksaw?*" Bertie gulped. "What for?"

The zookeeper laughed. "Well, if all else fails, we can chop off your head."

Dirty Bertie

"WHAT?" Bertie jerked his head back. To his surprise he suddenly found himself on the ground.

"YOU DID IT!" shouted Darren. "YOU'RE OUT!"

A cheer went up from the crowd. Bertie blinked. He didn't know how he'd done it but he was finally free.

The zookeeper helped him to his feet. "I was joking about chopping off your head by the way," he said with a wink.

Dirty Bertie

The class all crowded round Bertie, talking at once. This had definitely been the highlight of the day so far. Eugene and Darren gave Bertie high fives. Only Miss Boot didn't look thrilled.

"This is what comes of wandering off," she scolded. "From now on you will stay where I can see you – and DO NOT touch anything." She checked her watch. "I think it's time we stopped for lunch."

They found some picnic tables near the elephant house. Bertie took out his lunch box. All he had left was an apple, crisps and one measly cheese roll.

Know-All Nick sat down next to him. "Is that all you've got?" he sneered. "*I've* got crisps, sandwiches AND jam doughnuts."

"Lucky you," said Bertie.

One of the elephants lumbered out of its house to take a look at them. It gave Bertie an idea. Maybe he could still get even with clever-clogs Nick.

"Hey, Nickerless, why don't I take your picture?" he said.

Know-All Nick looked surprised. But he could never resist the chance to have his picture taken. He stood up, posing as if he was about to eat his doughnut.

"Too close," said Bertie. "Go back a bit."

"Like this?" asked Nick.

"No, back a bit more."

"Here?"

"Just a bit further!"

Nick stepped back until he found himself against a wall.

"Perfect," said Bertie. "Now hold the doughnut up. Higher!"

Nick did as he was told… Suddenly a hairy trunk shot over the wall and grabbed the doughnut.

"MISS!" wailed Nick. "THE ELEPHANT'S GOT MY DOUGHNUT!"

Miss Boot looked over. "Nicholas!" she yelled. "How many times? DO *NOT* FEED THE ANIMALS!"

Dirty Bertie

Bertie grinned as he snapped a picture.
Maybe in future this would teach Nick
a lesson – nobody made a monkey out
of him!